COPYT

A COPYCAT
DRAWING BOOK
by
Sally Kilroy

PUFFIN BOOKS

For Tom and Jack

A BUS

Draw a bus with two wheels, like this.

Then add windows, bumpers and lights.

Add a sign and a number, and colour it.

Now put a driver, conductress and passengers inside.

PEOPLE

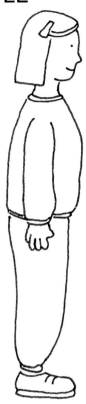

Try drawing
a sideview
like this.

WALKING

Swing the nearest
leg and the furthest
arm forward.

Then swing those ones
back and the others
forward.

BENDING

Draw a top half
leaning forward
like this.

Then add
a bottom half.

KNEELING

Draw the same top half,
but bend the legs
so she kneels.

RUNNING

Draw the top
of a person
leaning forward,
with his arm bent.

Keep him leaning, and try drawing him
first with one leg bent up, then the other one.

SITTING

When sitting, the top half of legs look very short.
People sometimes cross their feet, knees or arms.

A PIG

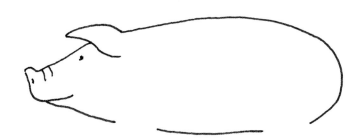

Draw a face
with a big wrinkly nose
and a floppy ear.

Add the body,

A SHEEP

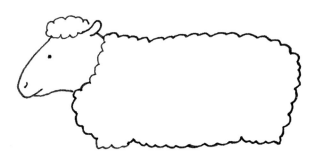

Draw a face like this,
with a little ear
and some wool on top.

Add a woolly body,

A GOAT

Draw a pointed face
with horns and
an ear.

It has a longer neck
and smaller body.
Add a beard.

Try drawing the animals from the front.

then legs, trotters (feet) and a curly tail.

They all have split feet.

then legs, hooves (feet), and a woolly tail.

Some sheep have horns.

Now draw thin legs with hooves
and a wispy tail.

The goat
has longer legs.

A TREE HOUSE

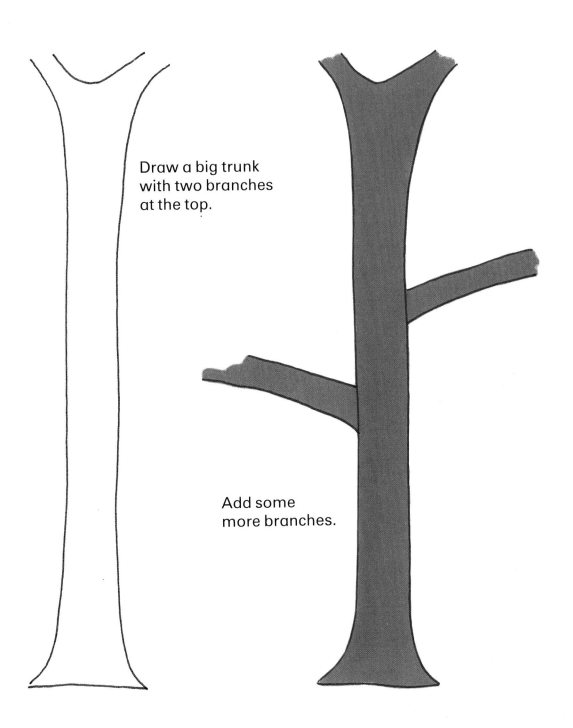

Draw a big trunk
with two branches
at the top.

Add some
more branches.

Use lots of blobs to draw clumps of leaves on the branches.

Draw a tree house on one branch.

Add a rope ladder and someone climbing up.

Someone else is having a swing.

A FISHING BOAT

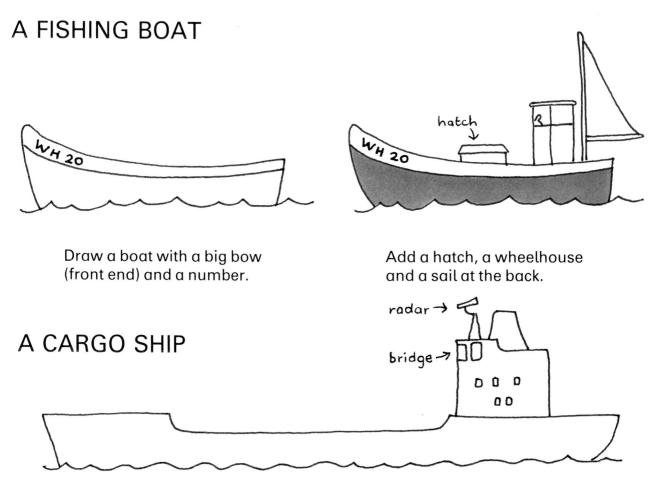

Draw a boat with a big bow
(front end) and a number.

Add a hatch, a wheelhouse
and a sail at the back.

A CARGO SHIP

Draw a very long ship, with radar and a funnel.
Add windows for the bridge and cabins.

A CAR FERRY

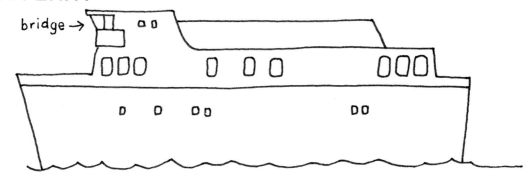

Draw a high ship like this with a bridge.
Put in some large and some small windows.

Put in the fishermen –
give one a net to pull in some fish.

Draw a lighthouse
on a rock in the water.

Now add a mast for lights, an anchor and a name.
Then load it with lots of containers full of cargo.

Add a mast, a funnel and lifeboats.
You could load some vehicles.

IN THE FARMYARD
A TRACTOR

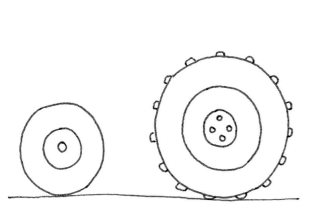

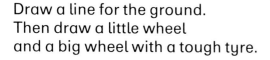

Draw a line for the ground.
Then draw a little wheel
and a big wheel with a tough tyre.

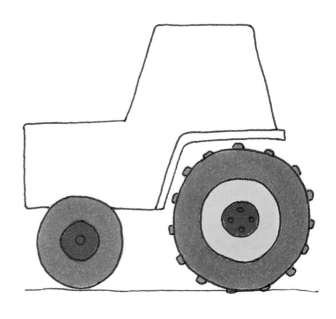

Add the front and the cab.
Draw a mudguard
over the big wheel.

Try a different-coloured tractor;
put in a farmer, and hook on a trailer
full of animals, hay or sacks.

Put in a door, a window
and a step.

Finish it with an engine,
an exhaust pipe and lights.

Add a farm building
to your picture,
with some straw bales inside.

You could draw someone
feeding chickens too.

A TORTOISE

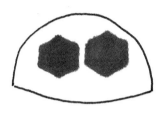 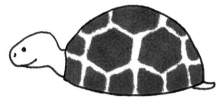 

Draw a shell
with this pattern.

Finish the pattern.
Add a head and tail.

Then some legs.

A RABBIT

Draw the head
with long ears.

Add an eye
and a body,

then legs and
a fluffy tail.

A FOX

Draw a pointed face
with pointed ears.

Then draw the body
and legs.

Give him
a long bushy tail.

BUTTERFLIES

Draw a head
with antennae,

then a body
in two parts.

Draw a big wing on
each side of the
big part of the body.

Then draw two more
wings, like this.

A FROG

Draw a face
with huge eyes.

Add a body
and little front legs.

Now draw the back legs
with long toes.

A DUCK

Draw a head
with a beak,
like this.

Now add the body
with a wing
and a little tail.

Stand him on webbed feet,
or float him on water.

A FUEL TANKER

Draw a cab and wheel base.

Add a tank of fuel, a sign and a flashing light.

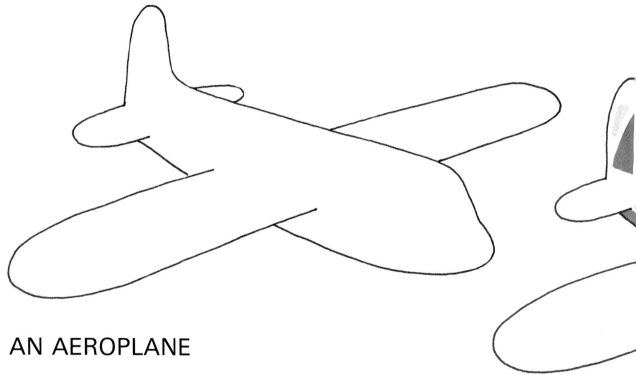

AN AEROPLANE

Draw an aeroplane like this.

Add engines, windows, a door with a stewardess, and the pilot.

A LUGGAGE TRAILER

Draw a buggy
with an empty trailer.

Put in a driver
and fill it with cases.

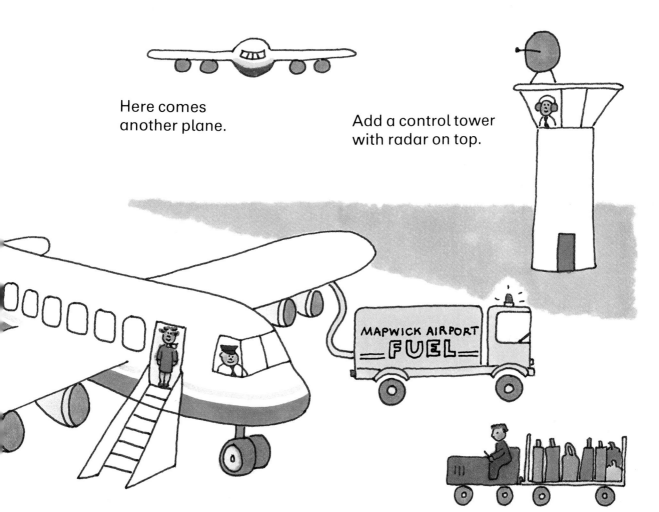

Here comes
another plane.

Add a control tower
with radar on top.

Put some steps
up to the door,
and add wheels
under the front.

Now draw a fuel tanker
filling up the plane
and a luggage trolley.

A CAFÉ

Draw a building like this.

Add an awning.

Then draw windows upstairs and a big door and window below.

A WAITER

Draw his face.

Add a shirt, bowtie and hands,

then an apron.

Now draw his trouser and shoes, and a tray with a drink.

Try some chairs and a table.

You could draw a big picture like this.

Add window boxes full of flowers.

Draw a sign with the café's name.

The Wild Mouse

CAFE

Some customers have arrived!

AT THE MARKET

Draw a table
with trestle legs, like this.

Put some scales on it
and draw a big umbrella behind.

A MEAT OR FISH VAN

Draw a van, like this.

Open the side and draw a man
selling meat or fish.

Now add lots of boxes
of fruit,

and a lady to sell it.

Don't forget to draw
some customers.

You can see the side
of this plant stall.

A HORSE OR PONY

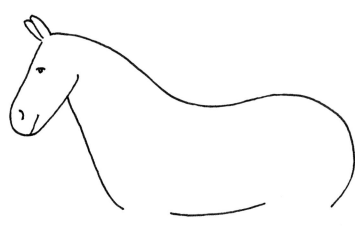

Draw a head
with an eye, nostril and mouth –
then the ears and neck.

Now add a slightly curved
back and tummy.
Draw round the bottom.

A RIDER

Draw a pony.
Put on a saddle and bridle.

Sit a rider on top,
with her foot in a stirrup.

Add the front legs
and hooves (feet),

then the
back legs and hooves.

Draw a mane
and tail.

Foals have fuzzy
manes and tails,
and long, thin legs.

TROTTING

Draw a head and body,
and two legs like this.

Add two more legs
swinging out behind and in front.

AT THE BEACH

Draw some heads and bodies.
Add arms and stand them in the water.

PLAYING BALL

  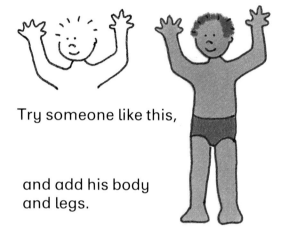

Draw the head
and arms,

then add the body
and legs.

Try someone like this,

and add his body
and legs.

GRANNY AND GRANDPA

Draw their heads
and bodies.

Then add their arms.

A RUBBER DINGHY

Draw a boat on the water.
Fasten an oar to it.

Put people with
lifejackets in it.

Put them on
the beach,
throwing a ball.

Now draw their legs, and sit them on towels.

Add a picnic basket,
a crab and shells.

TRAFFIC

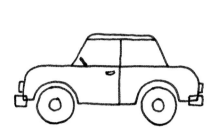

Here is a car.

Try one with a sunroof, towing a caravan.

Here is a lorry.

Put something in it, and add a driver.

A jeep is this shape. Hitch on a horse box.

Oh dear!
Roadworks.

People are crossing
at the traffic lights.

An estate car looks
like this at the back.

This one is towing
a speedboat.

A policeman
is directing
the traffic.

Draw a van.

Now make it
an ice-cream van.

A breakdown truck
has a flashing light,

a winch and a hook.

The car is
'ON TOW'.

A SHARK

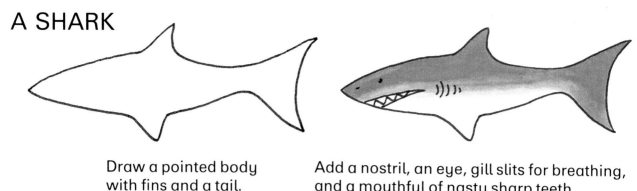

Draw a pointed body with fins and a tail.

Add a nostril, an eye, gill slits for breathing, and a mouthful of nasty sharp teeth.

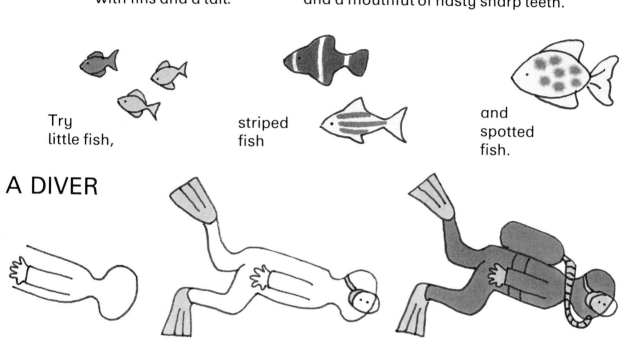

Try little fish,

striped fish

and spotted fish.

A DIVER

Draw a head, body, and arm, like this.

Add goggles, eyes and legs with flippers.

Strap on a tank of air with a pipe to his mouth.

AN OCTOPUS

Draw the head and eyes.

Now add four legs,

then another four.

SUNKEN TREASURE

Try making up a picture with a wreck and some treasure on the sea bed.
Have the divers seen the treasure . . . or the shark?

PEOPLE IN THE PARK

Draw a lady walking with arms forward, pushing a pram.

Bending to feed the ducks.

This is a three-quarters view, so you see most of her face, but not her other ear.

ROLLER SKATING

Draw someone skating, like this.

Draw him just the same, but tipping back and looking worried.

Now draw the same top but spread his legs to make him fall.

The people on the bench are smaller because they are further away.

This boy is leaning back and swinging up his leg to kick a ball.

This girl is leaning back and holding on to her kite.

A PARTY TEA

Draw a table with a big white cloth on it.
Add a cake and lots of nice things to eat.

Sit children in party hats round the table.
Give them cups, plates and food.